Good Little WOLF

Nadia Shireen

JONATHAN CAPE • LONDON

D0258243

04699599

Are we all sitting comfortably? Then let's begin . . .

Rolf and Mrs Boggins were best friends.
"You really are a good little wolf," Mrs Boggins told him.
Rolf liked being a good little wolf.

He liked baking
tasty cakes.

He ate up all
his vegetables.

And he was always
nice to his friends.

But Mrs Boggins also said that not *all* wolves were good. In fact, some were downright bad.

Rolf hoped he would never bump into a big bad wolf.

You SMELL like a wolf . . .?"

"That's because I AM a wolf," piped up Rolf.
"I'm a very good little wolf."

"Good?" said the Big Bad Wolf.
"Wolves aren't good!
Wolves are BIG and BAD."

"Real wolves howl at the moon!"
hooted the Big Bad Wolf.
"Real wolves blow houses in!
Real wolves eat people up!"

"Well," said Rolf. "I am a real wolf.
And I'm sure I can do all of
those things."

So Rolf tried to howl at the moon.

He pursed his lips, took a deep breath,
and out came a great big . . . whistle.

Then Rolf went to see Little Pig.

"Do you mind if I blow your house in?" asked Rolf.

"You can try, I suppose," said Little Pig.

So he huffed . . .

And he puffed . . .

But it was no use.

"I'm sorry, Rolf,"
said Little Pig.

"You're right!" said Rolf sadly.
"I'm just not bad enough to be
a real wolf."

"Well . . . there is one last thing you
can do to prove you're a proper wolf,"
said the Big Bad Wolf.

And suddenly, something quite
strange came over Rolf.

He felt an unfamiliar, wild feeling
growing inside him . . .

Rolf had never felt
more like a wolf.

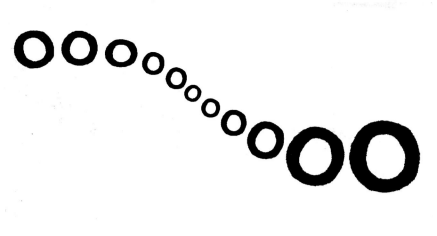

"See? I am a proper wolf.
I just happen to be a
GOOD little wolf," said Rolf.

"This calls for a celebration!" cried Mrs Boggins.
And they all sat down for some tea and cake.

"Will you stop eating people up,
Big Bad Wolf?" asked Rolf.

"Oh, I suppose so," said the Big Bad Wolf . . .

The end.

G O O D
LITTLE   WOLF
A   JONATHAN   CAPE   BOOK
978   1   780   08001   7   Published
in   Great   Britain   by   Jonathan   Cape,
an imprint of Random House Children's Books
A   Random   House   Group   Company
This edition published 2011   2 3 4 5 6 7 8 9 10
Copyright © Nadia Shireen, 2011   The right of Nadia Shireen
to be identified as the author of this work has been asserted
in accordance with the Copyright, Designs and Patents Act 1988.
All rights reserved.   RANDOM HOUSE CHILDREN'S BOOKS
61–63   Uxbridge   Road,   London   W5   5SA
www.kidsatrandomhouse.co.uk   www.rbooks.co.uk
Addresses for companies within The Random House Group
Limited can be found at: www.randomhouse.co.uk/offices.htm
THE RANDOM HOUSE GROUP Limited Reg. No. 954009
A   CIP   catalogue   record   for   this   book   is
available   from   the   British   Library.   Printed
in   China.   With   huge   thanks   to
my   tutors   and   friends   at
Cambridge   School   Of   Art,
A   R   U   .

For my mum and in memory of my dad. With love x